Dog Stories

Tales of the Hero Dog Max

D1607671

Grace Kenny

Table of Contents

Foreword..1

STORY 1 Forever Forward: 3

    Chapter 1 4

    Chapter 2 7

    Chapter 3 10

    Chapter 4 13

    Chapter 5 17

STORY 2 Paws of Courage: 20

    Chapter 1 21

    Chapter 2 25

    Chapter 3 28

    Chapter 4 32

    Chapter 5 34

STORY 3 From Strangers to Lifesavers: 37

    Chapter 1 38

    Chapter 2 40

    Chapter 3 45

STORY 4 Scent of Hope: 47

    Chapter 1 48

    Chapter 2 51

STORY 5 HEROES AMONG US 54

    Chapter 1 55

    Chapter 2 58

    Chapter 3 61

    Chapter 4 64

Conclusion 67

Foreword

Growing up in a small village in rural Ireland, my world was an enchanting blend of tradition, storytelling, and the pure, unfettered love of dogs. From my earliest memories, dogs have been far more than pets to me; they have been my companions, my confidants, and my best friends.

Throughout my childhood, a parade of paw prints graced our home, and each of those beloved creatures became a part of our family. Even the neighbors' dogs were a regular presence, adding even more personality and welcoming chaos to our household. These dogs were my playmates during the day and guardians through the night. Their presence was as natural and necessary as the mist on a cool Irish morning.

This collection of short stories was born from the nostalgia I feel when I think of those days. Inspired by the dogs that have graced my life, I have crafted tales centered around a representation of the best parts of each dog - Max.

Max journeys through the narratives, a symbol of loyalty and love that represents the best parts of all the dogs I had the privilege of growing up with.

He embodies something genuinely heroic: the pure, unconditional love and enduring spirit of a dog. His actions, his instincts and, his unwavering love for his human counterparts—all these characteristics are stitched together from the memories of my own canine companions.

Creating this book has been a journey back to the streets of my village, the roaring fires that battled the chill in our old house, and the wagging tails that greeted me every day after school. Each story is a tribute to the incredible souls who taught me about loyalty, love, and the irreplaceable joy that a dog can bring into one's life. These memories are condensed into Max, a collection of tales that, I hope, will speak to everyone who has loved and been loved by a dog.

In these pages, you will find a piece of my heart, the echo of my past, and the dogs—especially Max—that made me who I am today. These stories are my gift to them, a humble offering of gratitude for the immeasurable happiness they brought into my life.

As you journey through these tales, may you too experience the warmth of Max's presence, and may he guide you through the vibrant, rolling meadows of love, loyalty, and life itself that he has come to symbolize.

- *Grace Kenny*

STORY 1

Forever Forward:

The Unlikely Partnership of a

Wounded Soldier and a Spirited Dog

Chapter 1

In the heart of the night, under the shroud of darkness, Captain Brett Stratton and a small team of soldiers moved with measured steps through the hostile terrain. The air was thick with tension, each breath they took was weighed down by the gravity of their mission. The moonlight whispered over the landscape, casting eerie shadows that seemed to dance with the very shadows of danger they sought to evade.

As they trudged through the darkness, their precarious situation became more apparent. They were only a few minutes away from their extraction point. But to get there, they had to go through the most dangerous areas of their mission so far. Every step they took was deliberate, every movement was calculated. Hours earlier, they had painstakingly marked the route, carefully avoiding the treacherous landmines hidden beneath the soil. The memory etched into their minds, a constant reminder of the deadly threat they faced.

The night was still, almost unnaturally so. The rustle of leaves, the crunch of boots against the ground—each sound seemed to reverberate through the silence, a warning that any misstep could spell disaster. Their progress was painfully slow. Every inch they gained was a small victory against the unknown dangers hidden in the shadows.

But suddenly, fate dealt them a terrible hand. Someone stumbled. It was only a slight misstep—not much. The faintest sound resonated in the air, a chilling note of impending doom. Time seemed to freeze for a heartbeat before the night erupted into chaos.

Bullets pierced the silence of the night air, a hail of gunfire rained down on them. The very shadows that had concealed them now seemed to reveal their presence to the enemy, the element of surprise lost in a storm of lead. Survival suddenly became the team's number one goal as soldiers began to drop under the onslaught. Captain Brett Stratton fired off instructions and warnings simultaneously as all who were still standing sought cover. Amid the chaos, he lunged forward instinctively, his body acting as a shield to push a teammate out of the path of an oncoming bullet. He felt, more so than saw, the shot coming and acted instinctively.

The bullet's impact unleashed an avalanche of agony that swept through his entire being with an unrelenting force. His vision blurred, his ears rang with the echo of the gunshot, and time seemed to slow to a crawl. Still in the throes of agony, he caught sight of something that sent a shock of terror through him – the glint of a landmine beneath his feet.

To his right another soldier was scrambling to his feet.

Brett's heart pounded like a war drum, the furious rhythm drowning out the chaos around him. In a split second that seemed to stretch into eternity, he grappled with the knowledge that every movement could be his last. The cold sweat on his brow mingled with the searing heat of pain from the gunshot wound as he realized how close he was to death's door.If the bullets didn't kill him, the landmine surely would. In those few desperate seconds, he made a decision. With every ounce of strength he could muster, he propelled himself forward, throwing the soldier clear of the impending explosion.

The world became a whirlwind of sensations – blinding light, earth-shaking force, and the feeling of being torn apart.

For a few seconds, he felt weightless as his body was flung into the air by the force of the explosion but then slammed into the ground like a rag doll carelessly discarded into a corner at a child's whim. It was a fierce reminder that life was a fragile thing, and he clung to that rhythm even as his vision dimmed, and his consciousness slipped away. He heard his teammates calling to him, voices distant and indistinct, as though coming from a world far removed from his own. As the veil of unconsciousness wrapped around him, a wave of remorse washed over him. The realization hit him hard—he would never see his sister again. The thought alone sent shivers down his spine.

But that was not all. His responsibility to guide his men to safety weighed upon his soul like a heavy anchor. Their calls for help echoed in his mind, but he could not answer. He couldn't lead them out of danger; they were so close to safety. The reality before him was a bitter pill.

Images of his sister and his comrades flashed through his mind. His last coherent thought was a whispered apology to all of them for leaving them this way.

Was this his final bow? Was this his exit from a life dedicated to service and sacrifice? The question echoed in the recesses of his mind even as the darkness claimed him, his body succumbing to the numbing embrace of unconsciousness. And in that void, as the battlefield receded, a question loomed – had he failed?

Chapter 2

Captain Brett's eyes fluttered open; his senses still groggy from the haze of unconsciousness. The dim lights in the hospital room cast a gentle glow on the surroundings. Judging by the darkness he could see outside the window across from his bed; it was nighttime.

For a fleeting moment, he felt disoriented, the unfamiliar setting of the room and the distant sounds of murmurs echoing in his ears. He tried to piece together where he was and how he had gotten there.

As his awareness slowly sharpened, the memories flooded back, crashing over him like waves. The chaotic battle, the treacherous terrain, the unbearable pain of the bullet that had struck his side. The explosion, the deafening noise, and then, darkness.

Was he dead? Was he in some alternate universe where the rules of reality were different?

Brett's eyes scanned the room, taking in the outlines of the other patients in their beds. The soft breaths and occasional snores created a rhythmic backdrop to his racing thoughts. He squinted to make out the clock on the distant wall—3:00 AM. The world seemed surreal, an alternate reality where time had lost meaning.

A wave of relief washed over him, a profound sense of gratitude for simply being alive. In those final moments on the battlefield, he had been convinced that the breath he took before losing consciousness would be his last. But here he was, breathing, thinking, feeling.

His gaze flickered to the window, the pale light of the moon casting a silvery glow on the floor. His thoughts shifted to his men. How many had made it out? The fact that he was lying here, away from the landmine-ridden field, was a testament that some had survived. But how many? He couldn't shake off the worry gnawing at his heart.

With a conscious effort, he wriggled his fingers, the simple action helping to rekindle his connection with his body. A twinge of discomfort shot through his side, a painful reminder of the bullet's impact. He stilled, his fingers curling into a tight grip on the sheets. But the realization that he couldn't feel anything from the waist down was even more alarming.

He moved his gaze around the room, eventually landing on the lamp on the bedside table. A surge of determination welled up within him, and he reached out to turn it on. The harsh light flooded the softly lit room, momentarily blinding him. As his eyes adjusted, he cast his gaze downward, eager to get his first good look at himself.

The sheet covering his lower body seemed almost innocuous, but as he threw it off, he was met with a sight that struck him like a physical blow. A pile of bandages wrapped around his calves, but beyond that, emptiness stretched like a chasm. The shock was a heavy weight that settled into his chest, his mind struggling to process the enormity of what he was seeing.

"No!" he whispered, his voice trembling, the word escaping his lips before he even realized. It was as if time slowed down, and he found himself caught in a waking nightmare. Denial surged through him, an immediate, almost instinctual refusal to accept the truth his eyes were delivering.

The reality began hammering in his mind like a relentless drumbeat, and with each passing second, it grew louder until the anguish spilled through his lips. His desperate, agonized wails suddenly pierced the silence of the night. He clawed at the bandages, his fingers tearing at them as if they made of fire.

The lights in the room seemed to intensify, their glare a stark contrast to the darkness that seemed to envelop him. Voices swirled around him, attempting to calm him and get through the haze of shock and pain. Hands reached out, trying to restrain him, to guide him away from the grip of his own despair.

But in that moment, Brett felt a wild desperation, a raw, primal need to escape the reality that had shattered his world. The hands that sought to comfort him became obstacles, their touch igniting a frantic need to free himself from the confines of his anguish.

He fought against the hands that held him, his voice rising from a desperate whisper to a heart-rending scream. His throat burned with the effort, his vision blurring as he thrashed and struggled. More hands joined in, a cacophony of voices trying to break through to him, to pull him back from the precipice of his despair.

And then, like a crescendo building to its peak, the world began to fade. The hands, the voices, the blinding lights—all merged into a disorienting whirlpool. The pain, the heartache, the shock—they all seemed to meld together, becoming a muffled symphony as darkness once again beckoned him. As the world around him slipped away, the same question that plagued him on the battlefield returned: Was he bowing out of life and service as a failure?

Chapter 3

The soft hum of hushed voices filled the hospital room, a delicate symphony Brett's ears latched onto as he hovered between slumber and consciousness. He kept his breathing steady, feigning sleep as he allowed the conversation from the next bed to wash over him. Every word, every whisper, held an intimate weight that tugged at his senses.

"Six men," a voice murmured, a mixture of awe and concern lacing the words. "That's how many it took to restrain him. I honestly felt his pain as I watched the entire scene play out."

Brett's heart clenched at the realization that others had witnessed the events from earlier. His fingers twitched slightly, the instinctive reaction threatening to betray his facade of slumber. He remained still, his body unmoving, his ears attuned to every nuance of the conversation.

A different voice chimed in, "A couple of other patients in this room shed tears for him. Captain Brett Stratton, that's his name. The dude's a great guy and an incredible leader. He's repeatedly stood up for his men, protected them, and led them through dangerous terrain."

Brett felt a mixture of pride and vulnerability at the words spoken about him. The memories of those missions—the treacherous landscapes, the life-threatening situations, and the unwavering camaraderie with his team—flashed through his mind. He had always believed in being a shield for his men, to lead from the front and make sure they always made it out safely. But now, lying wounded and broken, he wondered if his leadership had been enough.

Then a sombre tone entered the conversation, accompanied by a sigh. "It's such a shame, you know. So unfair that fate chose to treat him this way. Just unfair."

The heaviness of those words settled over Brett like a shroud. Unfair—yes, that was the word that had been echoing through his thoughts ever since he had awoken in this unfamiliar room. His fingers clenched into fists beneath the sheet, hidden from view as he struggled to contain the emotions that surged within him.

And then, a new voice—a soft, delicate timbre, a counterpoint to the sadness that hung in the air—whispered, "But he's alive."

The simple statement was like a lifeline, a reminder that there was still a spark of hope amidst the darkness. Brett turned his head away from the sound of the voices, his cheeks wet with tears he hadn't realized had fallen. He was grateful for the cover of his feigned slumber, hiding the turmoil that threatened to spill forth.

Another speaker's voice, touched by empathy, responded in a low murmur, "That's relative, my dear. For a soldier, some things are just more painful than death."

Brett's heart clenched at the truth in those words. He understood them all too well. The loss of his legs, the shattered dreams of returning to the battlefield, the weight of feeling like he had somehow failed his men—it was a pain that ran deeper than any physical wound.

Emotions overwhelmed him, causing his breathing to catch and his tears to flow faster. He sought refuge in the hospital bed, his face buried in the soft sheets. In this moment of vulnerability, he grappled with the immense grief that threatened to consume him.

Amidst the relentless grip of his emotions, Brett's heart was a cavern of

11

desolation. He was trapped in a vortex of agony, a prisoner to the torment that had consumed his very being. The voices that floated around him were distant echoes, meaningless whispers that held no solace, only a cruel reminder of the world he had been thrust into.

Alive, they said. The word reverberated in his mind, a mocking echo that taunted his shattered existence. What did it matter? What use was life when he was chained to a body that had betrayed him, when every breath he took was a testament to his anguish?

He yearned to scream and release the torrent of agony that had consumed him, but the abyss that had claimed him had taken even his voice.

He was a warrior, a captain who led his men with courage and honor. But now, as he lay immobilized, his spirit was a phantom, a specter of the man he used to be. The battlefield had been his realm, his domain, where courage reigned supreme. Now, in this sterile hospital room, he was nothing but a casualty, a fragment of the hero he had once been.

Chapter 4

Eighteen months later.

Brett stared at the glass case above the mantle in his living room, where his sister had displayed all the decorations he had received throughout his service years. Ten years in all.

It felt as though they all belonged to another existence, a distant era. His life now was completely different.

After his discharge from the hospital, he spent several months with his sister and her family. In those months, they pampered and sheltered him until he got fed up.

He yearned for a sense of independence, a life where he wasn't a constant recipient of others' care.

Throughout his recovery, Brett had received various forms of assistance, including therapy and equipment like the electric wheelchair that was now a part of his daily life. It was both a blessing and a stark reminder of the irreversible changes he had endured. After leaving his sister's home, he moved into a small house, and though his body still bore the scars of his past, he kept himself busy fixing things around his home. The physical labour served as a form of therapy, helping him regain a sense of purpose and accomplishment.

Despite his progress, the nightmares lingered, a haunting reminder of the horrors he had experienced. He knew that healing took time, and he had learned to accept the process, even if it meant confronting his demons during sleep.

A thought struck Brett like a lightning bolt as he continued staring at the glass case. He needed to make a shift if he ever wanted a semblance of a life beyond his current state. He needed to step out of his comfort zone, away from the familiar surroundings that both nurtured and confined him.

The idea of escaping, of going somewhere nobody knew or expected anything from him, began to take shape in his mind.

With newfound determination, Brett picked up the phone and started making arrangements. He contacted his sister, Grace, to let her know he had something important to discuss with her. She was enthusiastic over the phone, mentioning that she also had a surprise for him. Brett chuckled softly, appreciating the sibling bond that remained unbreakable despite the passage of time and distance. They promised to catch up later that day.

When Grace arrived at his doorstep, she had a dog carrier in her hand.

Brett took one look at the carrier, and the word "No!" exploded out of his mouth. His heart raced at the unexpected turn of events. His initial response was a mix of concern and disbelief—how could he possibly care for another living being when he could barely care for himself?

Grace, always perceptive, smiled gently and placed a hand on his shoulder. "Brett, I know it's a big step, but hear me out," she said. "Responsibility has a way of propelling us forward. Caring for another can help you discover new strengths in yourself."

Brett sighed, his gaze falling to the ground. "I'm already trying to find my way forward, Grace. I've made arrangements to take some time away, to clear my head and figure things out."

Grace's expression softened. "And that's exactly why this could be good for you. It's not just about taking care of the dog; it's about taking care of yourself in a different way. You're capable of more than you realize."

Brett's internal struggle was evident in his eyes. He appreciated his sister's perspective, but the weight of his own limitations was heavy on his shoulders. "Thank you for the offer Grace, and for the dog," he began, "but right now, I don't think I'm ready for this."

Grace nodded as she followed him into the house, her smile unwavering. "I understand Brett. I'll always support you, whatever you decide. And if you need anything, you know I'm just a call away."

During her visit, they talked about the details of his trip and the arrangements that needed to be made.

At some point, Grace excused herself to use the restroom. As Brett waited for her to return, his mind raced with conflicting emotions. But after waiting for what felt like an eternity, he grew concerned and decided to go looking for her.

Instead of finding his sister, he found a note resting on the hallway table. It simply read, "Sorry Bro" with a kiss imprinted below it.

Brett's heart tightened with a mix of emotions, and he was far from pleased with his sister's audacious move. He reached for his phone and attempted to call her, but the call went straight to voicemail. Frustration crept in as he left a terse message.

He returned to the living room, his gaze drawn to the dog carrier that now seemed to contain a hopeful golden retriever and a plethora of conflicting emotions. The dog's eyes, filled with curiosity and anticipation, met Brett's. Those eyes seemed to hold a silent plea, a message that transcended words, echoing, "Please, let me out."

Brett's frown deepened; his resolve wavered with the intensity of the dog's gaze. His lips formed a reluctant line as he finally sighed, giving in to a momentary lapse in his determination. "Just for a bit," he murmured under his breath, his voice a mixture of resignation and uncertainty. He opened the carrier's door, and the golden retriever emerged, tentatively stepping into the room as if testing the waters of his newfound freedom.

A card was attached to the side of the carrier, and Brett pulled it down to read it. The dog's name was Max, a name that seemed to carry its own weight of significance. Max was a few months old, a golden retriever with a love for adventure. The card contained details about Max's health record, shots, and other care-related information. Max's food and other things will be arriving any moment now. His sister had indeed taken care of everything, leaving Brett to grapple with the unexpected responsibilities that now lay before him.

Turning to look at Max, who had settled comfortably on the sofa, Brett couldn't help but wonder what his next move should be. Should he attempt to return Max? The logistics of that decision remained unclear, and Brett felt a mixture of apprehension and confusion. He found himself talking to the dog, his voice laced with uncertainty. "So, what should I do with you, Max?"

The dog's ears perked up at the sound of his name, an uncanny understanding shining in his eyes. With a graceful jump, Max trotted over to Brett, finding his way onto his lap. The dog looked up at him with a gaze that seemed to convey both patience and knowledge. It was a look that seemed to say, "You already know the answer, buddy. Why are you fighting it?"

A chuckle unexpectedly burst from Brett's lips at the dog's unspoken commentary. It was a moment of levity that pierced through the weight of his thoughts. In that instant, as he met Max's gaze, he felt something he hadn't felt in a long time—hope. The ember of optimism flickered within him, casting a warm light that began to push back the shadows of doubt and despair.

It was a small step, but it was a step, nonetheless. And as Max looked up at him with those soulful eyes, Brett knew that maybe, just maybe, this shift in his life wasn't entirely unwelcome.

Chapter 5

Over the course of the next three months, Brett's life underwent a transformation that even he couldn't have anticipated. What had started as an unexpected and slightly reluctant partnership with Max quickly blossomed into a bond that reshaped his perspective on life.

Brett's vacation took him to a serene coastal town, far removed from the hustle and bustle of his previous life. The salty sea air seemed to hold a promise of renewal and a chance for him to find some semblance of peace amidst the turmoil that had defined the last 18 months. Max, his loyal companion, was by his side every step of the way, his joyful presence becoming a balm to Brett's wounded soul.

At first, Brett's days were filled with cautious exploration. He and Max would walk along the beach, Max's tail wagging with unbridled enthusiasm as he raced against the waves and fetched sticks with an unquenchable zest for life. Max's exuberance was contagious and it was impossible to resist. Slowly but surely, Brett found himself joining in, his laughter mingling with the crash of the waves.

The simple pleasure of throwing a stick for Max soon turned into elaborate games of fetch, where other dogs and their owners joined in the fun. People who loved their four-legged companions were all around Brett, who once thought he had lost his ability to connect with others.

Conversations flowed easily as they exchanged stories about their dogs, lives, and dreams. But that was not all.

A special connection began to form between Max and another golden retriever named Luna.

Luna belonged to a couple named Lucy and David, who told him they frequently visited the beach with their lively companion. The bond that developed between Max and Luna was undeniable. They chased each other along the shoreline and shared toys. Their playfulness became infectious, drawing the attention of those around them.

Brett couldn't help but notice how Lucy and David often exchanged knowing glances whenever Max and Luna were together. As the weeks went by, he found himself engaged in conversations with the couple, discovering common interests and sharing stories of their dogs' escapades. Lucy and David's easy camaraderie reminded Brett of the connections he had forged with teammates back in the army.

Max, ever the intuitive companion, seemed to sense when Brett needed a moment of solitude or when he was ready to engage with others. The dog's boundless energy and easy-going nature became a bridge that connected Brett to his surroundings. It wasn't just about Max's presence; it was about the connections he forged on Brett's behalf.

As the days turned into weeks, Brett's laughter became more frequent, and his heartache was slowly replaced by moments of genuine joy. Max's antics, his playful barks and affectionate nuzzles, became a constant source of amusement and comfort. There was a warmth in their companionship, a feeling of being understood without needing words.

One evening, as the sun set over the tranquil sea, Brett sat on the porch of his rented cottage, Max at his feet. The dog's head rested on his lap, and as Brett absentmindedly stroked his fur, he realized how much Max had changed his life. A sense of belonging had taken the place of the isolation that had plagued him.

Max had become more than a companion; he was a confidant, a steadfast friend who had guided him through the darkness that had threatened to consume him. With each passing day, Brett's heartache began to heal, and a new chapter in his life was unfolding—one defined by newfound hope and unexpected connections.

As Brett looked down at Max, who gazed up at him with eyes that seemed to hold wisdom beyond their age, he whispered words of gratitude. Max's presence had not only given him companionship but had also shown him that even in the face of adversity, there was still the possibility for joy and connection.

Later that evening, as Brett lay in bed with Max curled up beside him, his mind drifted back to the interactions with Lucy and David. He pondered the possibility of finding companionship again, a connection beyond friendship—with a partner who understood the scars he carried. One day, perhaps.

Over the last few days of his time away, Brett said his goodbyes to the beach and to the new friends he had made. Before leaving, he and his newfound companions exchanged contact details and addresses, promising to keep in touch.

During the flight back home, Brett couldn't help but feel a sense of gratitude for the furry friend who had entered his life. Max had given him more than he could have ever imagined—a reason to laugh, a companion to share his days, and a reminder that even in the darkest of times, there was always a glimmer of light.

STORY 2

Paws of Courage:

A Story of Loyalty and Bravery

Chapter 1

Lucy and Max ventured into the woods, the sun casting dappled patterns through the thick canopy of leaves above. Max's tail wagged in rhythm with Lucy's cheerful chatter as they followed the winding trail deeper into the belly of nature's sanctuary. With each step, Lucy's voice held a lighthearted tone, a mix of anecdotes about Luna, musings about the scenery, and gentle encouragement for Max to stay close.

As Lucy continued to share her thoughts with Max, a subtle shift in the atmosphere caught her attention. The air had grown heavy, a sign of impending change. The rustling leaves whispered warnings of an approaching tempest. Lucy's eyes narrowed as she scanned the sky, her brows furrowing as the gentle breeze transformed into an assertive gust. The winds seemed to swell, howling through the trees like a swift and relentless pack of wolves closing down on their prey.

Lucy felt a chill crawl up her spine as the truth dawned on her: the storm had arrived earlier than expected. The hounds of nature were now loose; unfortunately, she and Max had been caught unprepared.

With determination etched across her face, Lucy moved faster, urging Max to keep up. They were about fifteen minutes from her home, or so she thought. She could feel the first droplets of rain splattering against her skin, and the wind tugged at her clothes as if trying to hold her back.

Max's ears perked up, his instincts sensing the shift in the weather. He glanced at Lucy, his eyes reflecting concern and trust. He trotted alongside her with renewed purpose.

Their hurried steps echoed through the woods, a reminder of the race against time. Lucy's heart pounded as she pushed through the undergrowth, her breath coming in short gasps. She glanced at Max, and their eyes locked for a moment. This brief exchange conveyed both her determination and his unwavering loyalty.

But then, in a cruel twist of fate, a root hidden beneath the foliage caught Lucy's foot. Her body pitched forward, and her voice caught in her throat as she reached out instinctively to brace her fall. The world seemed to slow down as her body collided with the ground, a sickening thud echoing in her ears.

The rain began to pour, drenching Lucy's form as she lay still on the forest floor. Pain radiated from her limbs, and the wind seemed to mock her vulnerability. She tried to call Max to let him know she was all right, but her voice faltered into a weak groan.

Max, sensing Lucy's distress, turned back to her with a mixture of worry and confusion. He approached her slowly, his tail no longer wagging but held low, his eyes fixed on her unmoving form. He nuzzled her gently, as if urging her to get up. But Lucy remained still, her eyes fluttering as her consciousness wavered.

The storm raged around them in, contrast to Lucy's limp form. Max's instincts battled within him. He wanted to stay by Lucy's side to protect her from the onslaught of rain and wind. But he also sensed the urgency of the situation, the need to seek help. After one last longing look and nudge at Lucy, he let out a mournful howl that echoed through the woods, a desperate call for aid.

One month earlier.

In the early morning hours, the faint glow of dawn seeped through the curtains of Grace and her husband's bedroom as they lay sleeping. However, the familiar sound of Grace's phone ringing abruptly interrupted their peaceful slumber. Groggily, she fumbled for her phone on the nightstand and answered it.

"Brett?" Grace's voice held a mix of surprise and sleepiness as she listened to her brother's voice on the other end of the line. "What's going on?"

Brett's voice was tinged with excitement as he explained, "Hey, sis, sorry to wake you up. I just wanted to let you know that I'll be heading to the airport for another trip today."

"So soon?" Grace sat up in bed, a mixture of concern and curiosity filling her expression. "You just got back from one not too long ago."

Brett chuckled, "I know, I know. But it's been three months since I got back. Time flies, huh?"

Grace rubbed her eyes, trying to shake off her drowsiness as she processed her brother's words. "Three months already? Well, where are you off to this time?"

A hint of excitement danced in Brett's voice as he shared, "Actually, it's a bit spontaneous. Do you remember that couple I told you about, the one I met during my vacation? They invited me and Max to their hometown, and I thought, why not?"

Concern flickered across Grace's face as she imagined her brother embarking on another journey. She knew how much his previous vacation had meant to him, how it had brought back a spark of life that his past experiences had dimmed. "Brett, are you sure about this? You've been through so much."

But Brett's voice was resolute as he replied, "I am, Grace. Trust me, this is different. I've found something out there that's helping me heal, helping me find a way back to who I used to be."

Grace heard the sincerity in his words and felt a mixture of emotions. Her brother had been through unimaginable pain. If this journey was helping him find a sense of purpose and happiness again, she couldn't deny him that opportunity. With a sigh, she relented and said, "Okay,

Brett. If you're sure about this, I won't stop you."

She could hear the smile in Brett's voice as he replied, "Thanks, Grace. I appreciate your support."

She chuckled softly, with a hint of playfulness in her tone. "Just promise me you won't get into any crazy situations out there."

Brett laughed, the sound was genuine and lighthearted. "I'll do my best, sis."

Chapter 2

Upon his arrival at Lucy and David's town, Brett found Lucy, David and Luna waiting for him, their eager smiles matching the anticipation in his heart. As he rolled his wheelchair towards them, Max trotting along happily by his side, he felt a sense of familiarity and genuine warmth. It was as if no time had passed since their last meeting.

The exchange of warm hugs and joyful pleasantries came effortlessly, embodying the connections they had formed when they met at their vacation spot. Luna's tail flopped around wildly as she greeted Max, her excitement mirrored in the joyful barks that filled the air. The two dogs picked up their companionship right where they had left off, their playful antics a testament to their unbreakable bond.

After exchanging heartfelt greetings, they gathered Brett's and Max's luggage, loading it into the car with ease. They started the drive back home, the atmosphere full of companionable chatter, a mixture of catching up and cheerful banter that seamlessly flowed among them. Brett felt a blanket of comfort settle over him, as if he were returning to a place where he truly belonged.

As they drove through the town, Brett couldn't help but take in his surroundings. The town was smaller and more intimate than the bustling city he had come from, and its charm was undeniable. The community's peaceful ambience and laid—back nature were a stark contrast to the fast-paced life he was used to.

He listened attentively as David and Lucy pointed out key landmarks, important buildings, and notable locations, offering him insights into the heart of their town.

"It's a close-knit community," David explained, his voice carrying a sense of pride. "Everyone knows each other here."

Lucy chimed in, her eyes alight with enthusiasm. "And you'll find that everyone is always willing to lend a helping hand."

Brett nodded appreciatively, his gaze shifting from the quaint buildings to the lush surroundings. There was a sense of serenity in the air, a feeling he had been craving without realizing it. As they continued their drive, Brett couldn't help but feel a growing sense of connection to the town and its people.

As they reminisced about their past experiences and shared their hopes for the future, laughter and stories filled the journey. Max and Luna's playful energy in the backseat added to the cheerful atmosphere, a reminder of the joy of simple moments of companionship.

As the car made its way through the town's charming streets, Brett found himself drawn to the beauty of the landscape and the genuine connections surrounding him. He felt a sense of gratitude and hope for the beautiful days ahead in this welcoming and serene town.

Over the next few weeks, Brett spent his time in Lucy and David's town on a whirlwind of activities and new adventures. They took him under their wing, eager to share the beauty of their hometown with their newfound friend.

Lucy and David showed Brett the sights from sunrise to sunset, each location more captivating than the last. They strolled through quaint streets lined with charming shops and cozy cafes, the town's history unfolding before Brett's eyes with every step.

Moving from historical landmarks to scenic viewpoints, each place they visited held a story, and Lucy and David enthusiastically narrated it. They introduced him to the local cuisine, treating him to mouthwatering dishes with the region's flavors. Brett savored every bite, his taste buds coming alive with the unique blend of spices and ingredients that the town was known for.

Max and Luna joined them for these excursions, their presence adding to the sense of companionship and adventure. They explored the town together, forming a tight-knit group that drew curious looks and warm greetings from the locals.

As they ventured from one place to the next, Brett met many of the town's residents. Lucy and David's warm introductions made him feel like he was part of the community. The community welcomed him with open arms and showered him with gifts, especially when they realized he was also a veteran. By the end of the first week, he noticed that people were addressing him by his name, a testament to the tight-knit nature of the town.

As the days turned into weeks, Brett felt his heart open up to the connections he was forming. He exchanged stories and laughter with newfound friends, listened to tales of local legends, and shared his own experiences with an openness that had become second nature.

There was a sense of unity among the people, a shared bond that transcended their differences. The town even had a search and rescue center that trained humans and dogs, showcasing their commitment to community safety and preparedness.

Chapter 3

Present day.

Earlier that day, Brett took a deep breath as he moved the last box into David's car and hit the button. The trunk closed with a satisfying thud, a sense of accomplishment mingling with the unease in his chest.

He had been in this town for just a month. Life had settled into a pleasant rhythm. The bonds he had formed with Lucy, David, and the townspeople had grown more robust with each passing day. The warm community had begun to feel like a second home to him.

However, two days ago, a sense of urgency filled the air. A storm alert rang out, spreading throughout the town like wildfire. A storm was on the horizon, and all residents needed to prepare. They all had about forty-eight hours to secure their homes and gather supplies.

Brett, Lucy, David, Max, and Luna sprang into action, understanding the importance of heeding the warning.

Just a few hours later, the situation had escalated. Meteorological readings indicated that the storm was intensifying faster than anticipated. The winds were picking up speed, and the rain was becoming torrential. Panic rippled through the town as the reality of the impending storm set in. An updated alert advised all residents to seek shelter immediately, directing them to the closest communal storm shelters.

Gathering their essentials and important documents, they all rushed to prepare to move to the storm shelter. The atmosphere was tense, and anxiety hung heavy in the air. They knew the storm was no longer a distant threat—it was rapidly approaching, and their safety depended on their ability to act swiftly.

About twelve hours before the storm was expected to hit the town, Brett realized something crucial. Max had never experienced a situation like this before. He had never been confined or sheltered during a storm. On the other hand, Luna had been through these scenarios and was familiar with the routine.

As the men focused on the final preparations, Brett felt concerned for Max's well-being. He knew the storm shelter might be stressful for his furry friend. Max needed a walk—a chance to stretch his legs and release some pent-up energy before being cooped up.

Lucy saw the worry in Brett's eyes and understood without him having to say a word. She offered to take Max for a quick walk, promising to return quickly so they could all head to the shelter together. Brett agreed, trusting her with Max.

With a nod and a thankful smile, Lucy leashed up Max and set off for a brisk walk, her presence bringing comfort to the loyal dog.

The plan was simple: as soon as Lucy and Max returned, they would join the men, and they would all make their way to the storm shelter, where safety awaited them.

Now that he had loaded the last box, all that was left was for Lucy to return, and they would be on their way.

"Why is it taking her so long?" he muttered. "Hadn't it been long enough?"

As he turned to wheel his chair back into the house, David burst out of the front door to announce that Lucy had again forgotten to take her mobile phone.

An hour later, Lucy still hadn't returned. An unusual silence settled between the men, both unwilling to voice their fears. The sky overhead was growing darker, clouds were gathering in an ominous dance, and the wind carried a premonition of the storm's imminent arrival.

David's internal struggle was palpable, torn between staying with Brett and Luna and heading out to find his wife. He could sense Brett's unease as they heard the first rumbles of thunder. Finally, Brett's voice broke through the tension as he gently suggested that David drop him and Luna off at the community center first. It was a tough decision, but it made sense for David to focus on finding Lucy as quickly as possible and enlisting the help of others if necessary. They exchanged a determined nod, a silent pact made in the face of uncertainty.

Minutes later, David's car sped towards the community center, his knuckles white as he gripped the steering wheel. As they approached the center, he quickly maneuvered into a parking spot and practically leapt out of the car. Brett and Luna were just steps behind him, and the atmosphere around them was charged with concern and mounting dread.

As they entered the community center, some people noticed Lucy's absence and inquired about her whereabouts. David's voice was laced with worry as he explained that Lucy had taken Max for a walk but hadn't returned. His eyes scanned the room, searching for any sign of her, his heart pounding with anxiety.

A sudden burst of commotion echoed through the room as the conversation escalated. Someone rushed into the shelter and shouted that the storm alert had changed. The storm was close and would hit within the next two hours.

The announcement hung heavy in the air for a few seconds, a reminder that time was running out, and a sense of unease rippled through the room like a tidal wave.

Without a second thought, David dashed towards his car, his movements swift and determined. He knew he couldn't wait, not with the storm looming so close. Two other men, their expressions mirroring David's urgency, jumped into a nearby truck and revved the engine, ready to follow him.

Inside the community center, the atmosphere shifted as people's expressions turned from concern to palpable tension. Some residents ushered Brett and Luna further into the spacious center; their efforts were meant to provide comfort. People muttered reassurances that both Lucy and Max would soon return. The room grew quieter as the first signs of darkening skies appeared outside the windows. The once-joyful atmosphere now carried the weight of uncertainty, with each passing minute marked by the ticking clock and the gathering storm outside.

In that moment, the entire town united in a shared hope, their thoughts and wishes converging on Lucy and Max's safety and the collective prayer that the impending storm would spare their loved ones.

Chapter 4

Amid the swirling chaos in the woods, Lucy's consciousness flickered back to life as if fighting against the darkness that threatened to engulf her. Her vision was blurred, the world around her spinning in a dizzying whirl.

Max was right by her side, his warm tongue licking her face with concern and his whines giving an urgent plea for her to wake up. She tried to move, to rise, but the world tilted and spun, and a searing pain shot through her right leg. With a gasp, she collapsed onto the ground, her breath ragged as tears welled in her eyes.

Her right leg lay at an odd, twisted angle, the realization hitting her like a punch to the gut. She had broken her leg during the fall!

Panic surged within her as she looked up at the dark skies, the winds now howling through the trees with an eerie, menacing intensity. The air filled with the ominous sound of branches snapping and the creaking of trees swaying dangerously. How much time had passed? The urgency of their situation intensified, and Lucy felt a surge of terror grip her heart. She knew the storm was upon them, and she and Max were caught defenseless. Determination mingled with pain as she attempted to drag herself along the trail, every inch gained feeling like an eternity of agony. Max, her ever-present companion, stayed close, his worried eyes fixed on her, his whines a mixture of encouragement and concern.

The pain escalated with each movement until she finally had to stop. Max's whines grew more desperate, and he circled her, nudging her with his snout as if urging her to keep moving. Exhaustion and pain collided within her, and her body gave way to weakness. She turned to the side and vomited. The release of nausea only intensified her feelings of vulnerability and despair. Her sobs echoed through the woods as she clung to Max, seeking comfort in his unwavering presence.

Max, sensing her distress, continued his attempts to motivate her. He circled her, his eyes filled with a profound understanding that transcended words. He gently grabbed her wrist in his jaw, his eyes locking onto hers, his message clear: You're not alone; I'm here with you. She smiled weakly through her tears and whispered, "I hear you, buddy, but I can't move anymore."

Her strength was waning, the pain had become unbearable, and her consciousness once again flickered like a candle in the wind, but Max's devotion never wavered. He paced a few feet away, then back again, in a dance of urgency and desperation. With an almost supernatural intelligence, he reached out for the hoodie of her sweatshirt with his teeth as if intuitively knowing what he needed to do. He began to pull, his tugs gentle yet insistent, as if trying to guide her to safety.

Max's efforts continued relentlessly, even as the rain began to fall, drenching him. He switched between tugging on her hoodie and howling, his cries echoing through the woods, carrying an unspoken plea for help with them. His eyes locked onto the road they had left behind, a beacon of hope amid the chaos. His instincts, loyalty and everything else within him focused on getting Lucy out of harm's way. The roaring winds, pelting rain, and objects tossed about scared Max. However, his determination to protect Lucy remained unyielding, further strengthening his resolve. He tugged on Lucy's hoodie and howled, his voice rising above the din of the storm, and each tug a resounding declaration of his unwavering devotion to her.

Chapter 5

As the storm raged on, the men regrouped by the road where Lucy often walked, their voices raised to combat the howling wind that threatened to drown out their words. With determination etched across their faces, they quickly devised a plan to split up and cover more ground while staying within shouting distance due to the storm's interference with their communication. They dispersed while shouting encouragement, the gusts carrying their calls away.

They combed through the area, their voices carrying hope and desperation as they called out for Lucy and Max. The rain soaked them to the bone, and the cold wind cut through their clothing, but their determination burned brightly. After what felt like an eternity, they converged again, their faces laced with worry. David's heart ached as he realized the storm was intensifying and time was running out.

Amidst the rising storm, David remembered another path that Lucy occasionally frequented. With determination renewed, they piled into their vehicles and drove carefully through the increasingly treacherous conditions. Just meters away from their destination, a heavy branch slammed into David's windshield, causing his car to swerve uncontrollably before coming to an abrupt halt against a tree. The men rushed to his aid, their concern for his safety palpable.

Quickly abandoning the car, they squeezed into the truck and resumed their journey. Rain poured relentlessly, impairing their vision, yet a flicker of movement on the road ahead caught their attention. Struggling to see through the downpour, they strained their eyes until the figure became clear—Max.

His loyal heart was leading him to safety as he pulled Lucy along.

The realization hit them like a lightning bolt, and their breaths caught in their throats.

"Max!" one of the men whispered in awe.

"And he's pulling!" the other man exclaimed, his voice catching with emotion.

"Oh my God!" David finished, his voice barely a breath as he flung open the truck's door, his heart pounding with anticipation. The men stared in astonishment and wonder as they watched Max's determined efforts to bring Lucy to safety.

In that moment, amidst the tumultuous storm, Max stood as a beacon of unwavering devotion. As the rain soaked his fur, his eyes shimmered with determination and love. With every ounce of his strength, he pulled Lucy, his paws slipping on the wet road and his whimpers echoing in the wind. His actions were a testament to his boundless love for his companion, defying the odds and battling the elements to keep her safe.

As the men reached them, they gathered Lucy and Max into their arms, their tears mingling with the rain as they marveled at the incredible feat of loyalty and courage they had witnessed. It was a moment that transcended words, a silent acknowledgement of the remarkable bond between a human and her dog. Together, they rushed back to the car, their hearts swelling with gratitude for Max's heroic act.

Speeding towards the community center, the weight of worry began to lift, replaced by a sense of hope. On arrival at the center, local doctors and volunteers were on hand, ready to tend to Lucy's injuries with their expertise and compassion. Max, now a soggy and tired hero, rested beside Lucy, his tail thumping periodically on the floor as if to say, "I did it; I brought her back."

Amidst the storm's chaos, a profound truth emerged: love and courage can weather any tempest, and the unbreakable bond between a woman and her dog is a force of nature that transcends all obstacles.

STORY 3

From Strangers to Lifesavers:

Brett and Max's Journey to a New Life

Chapter 1

After the storm and Max's heroic act, the town came together to celebrate the bond between man and his faithful companion. Max's courage and unwavering devotion saved Lucy's life and touched the hearts of everyone who heard the tale. As a symbol of gratitude, the town council gave Max a medal as a token of recognition for his extraordinary deed. Max's tail spun in rapid circles as the medal settled around his neck, and the crowd cheered.

But the honor bestowed on Max didn't end there. The town recognized the incredible potential within Max's brave heart. It offered him a spot in their search and rescue program. It was a role perfectly suited for the courageous canine. This role allowed him to continue helping and protecting others. The town saw in Max not just a dog but a hero with a purpose. Max embraced his new role with the same unwavering determination he had shown on that fateful, stormy day.

As the days turned into weeks, Brett grappled with a decision tugging at his heart since the second week of his arrival. The connections he had formed with the people of the town, the warmth of their companionship, and the unwavering friendship he had found in Lucy and David—all of it had begun to weave itself into the fabric of his life. The town had welcomed him with open arms, embracing him as one of their own.

Brett looked around at the close-knit community, at the smiling faces of friends who had become family, and realized that his heart had already decided. The storm and Max's bravery had brought to light the undeniable truth: His future lay in this town with the townspeople and the bond he shared with Max.

So it was, with a mixture of anticipation and newfound purpose, that Brett decided to call the town his home. He knew that the road ahead would have challenges. Still, he was ready to take the plunge with the strength he had discovered within himself and the unwavering support of his new friends.

Max's bravery had not only saved Lucy's life; it had also opened the door to a new chapter in Brett's life.

As the seasons changed and the town moved forward, Brett became fully immersed in the rhythm of daily life. He contributed to the community in any way he could. He shared stories of his experiences and offered a helping hand whenever needed. Max joined the search and rescue team as a trainee and continued to exemplify courage and loyalty on every mission.

Brett's decision to stay had not only given him a sense of belonging but also given him a renewed sense of purpose. He realized that the town's laid-back charm, the genuine connections he had formed, and the unbreakable bond between Max and himself were all pieces of a puzzle that had finally come together. Looking out at the serene town, he couldn't help but feel that destiny had led him here, where a new chapter of his and Max's lives were unfolding.

Chapter 2

With a renewed sense of purpose, Brett seamlessly settled into the heart of the community he had come to cherish. Determination fueled his actions as he found a suitable house to remodel to accommodate his wheelchair and other needs. The process involved adjustments and renovations, but Brett was undeterred, knowing that this was a step towards making the town his permanent home. His sister, Grace, played an instrumental role in overseeing the shipment of his belongings from his previous residence, ensuring that his new environment would be as familiar and welcoming as possible.

In addition to securing a wheelchair-accessible home, Brett acquired a specially modified vehicle that allowed him to travel freely, further enhancing his sense of independence. With each stride, he constructed a life that aligned with his desires and ambitions – a life that gradually revealed itself as an extension of the journey he had embarked upon alongside Max.

One significant milestone was driving Max to the Search and Rescue center for the first time. A wave of gratitude washed over him as he navigated the roads with his loyal canine by his side. Max had given him a new avenue for giving back and serving, not on the same scale as his military service, but in a meaningful and impactful way. It was a chance to give back to the community that had embraced him and offered him a fresh start.

Arriving at the center, Brett met Mark, the person in charge of the canine division of the training program. Mark's warm welcome put Brett at ease as he introduced them to the bigger picture of the search and rescue program. Mark explained that the program aimed to train dogs like Max to assist in locating missing people or those stuck in dangerous situations that made it difficult for them to be found.

Mark led them through the facility, providing insight into the rigorous training regimen that the dogs underwent. The program included scent detection, obedience training, agility exercises, and simulated search scenarios to hone their skills. Brett listened attentively, his admiration for the program and its purpose growing with each passing moment. He recognized that this was his chance to contribute and to be a part of a team that helped safeguard the community in times of crisis.

As the tour continued, Brett's heart swelled with pride and gratitude. The center was a hub of purpose and dedication. It was a place where humans and dogs worked together for a common goal.

During the Search and Rescue center tour, Brett's anticipation grew as they approached the area where the handlers and their canine partners trained daily. A woman with midnight hair welcomed them as they entered the space, a bright smile illuminating her features. Her name was Eliora, a name Brett thought was well-suited to the beautiful woman.

She was to be Max's handler and partner in the search and rescue team.

For some reason, when Brett's hand met Eliora's in a handshake, he felt an inexplicable shift within him. It felt like a beginning, but he couldn't explain or understand his feelings.

But he did know that it was the first time in a long while that Brett felt a deep connection with another person apart from Lucy and David. And once again, it was all thanks to Max, the same faithful companion who had already changed the trajectory of his life.

Max's training allowed Brett to witness the remarkable journey of service animals, unveiling the profound depth of their skills. As someone who had seen a bit of the process in the military, Brett still marveled at the sheer dedication it took to elevate these animals to such levels of effectiveness. It was a revelation he'd never fully comprehended, and his respect for service animals rose to new levels.

Max's large stature undoubtedly granted him a natural advantage in certain areas. His robust physique and keen senses gave him an edge in various aspects of training. But there was much more to the process than mere size. It was a multifaceted endeavor that extended far beyond the surface.

It began with foundation training, where the handlers bonded with their dogs. Basic commands like sit, stay, and heel were the stepping stones for effective communication. Eliora and Max's partnership flourished during these initial stages, with the trust between them evolving into an unbreakable bond.

Socialization was another crucial aspect. Max's interactions with people, other dogs, and various environments honed his adaptability. This very skill enabled him to maintain his composure amidst the chaos of search and rescue missions.

Perhaps the most awe-inspiring aspect was Max's ability to differentiate scents.

His natural ability to discern scents climbed to incredible heights as he went through the training. He could pick up scents faster and farther than other dogs could and tell the difference between human scents and different scents.

This skill transformed him into a formidable tracker.

Max's large size came into play during the search technique training. He was a natural fit for wilderness searches. His sturdy build allowed him to traverse rugged terrains with ease. His agility defied his size, enabling him to navigate obstacles and remain sure-footed even in the most challenging environments.

Alerting behavior was the next phase, where Max mastered his unique signals. His deep bark and assertive stance became his means of communicating a discovery to Eliora. Their synchronization was a sight to behold—a harmonious blend of canine instinct and human guidance.

Navigation and direction training showcased Max's agility and response to commands. Eliora's cues guided him through a choreography of movements, a dance of trust and cooperation that translated into swift and coordinated searches.

Working on leash and off-leash was a testament to Max's discipline and focus. Whether tethered to Eliora or unbound, his dedication to the mission never wavered. His size, again, played a role—his presence commanded attention, a reminder of the importance of his abilities.

Mock search scenarios tested Max's abilities in lifelike situations. The complexity of these drills challenged his skills and adaptation, honing his ability to maneuver through ever changing scenarios. Max's large frame became an asset in situations that required him to support or assist in various tasks.

Advanced techniques were the final pieces of the puzzle, tailoring Max's training to specific tasks he might encounter. His training included water rescues and other specialized sessions to diversify his capabilities further.

As the training process culminated, Max emerged as a service dog and a vital lifeline in search and rescue operations. His large size, finely honed skills, and Eliora's expert guidance rendered him a beacon of hope for those in distress.

Max's itinerary settled into a predictable routine.

In the daytime, he and Eliora worked together, and later in the day, he would go home with Brett.

With his military background, Brett found himself fitting in naturally within the search and rescue organization, securing a role that utilized his skills while contributing to the search and rescue efforts.

In the days that followed, Both Brett and Max worked long hours. Max's training sessions were a testament to his undaunting commitment. On the other hand, Brett was frequently on the sidelines, watching as Max and Eliora went through the program and pushed themselves to excel.

The bond between Max and his handler deepened as they faced challenges together, drawing strength from their shared determination.

Max and Eliora progressed rapidly, and in about six months, Max was ready for the final assessment before his first official assignment.

As Brett observed the test from a distance, he remembered his final days in the military training camp with his mates. There were people he avoided after his injury because he didn't want to reopen old wounds.

But watching Max, he felt another part of the old resolve fade. He would reach out to those of his friends who were left. It was time they reconnected.

Max passed his assessment, and Brett couldn't have been happier for his buddy.

Chapter 3

Max's first assignment happened on a day that started as a typical day but, in the blink of an eye, was transformed into a pulse-pounding rush of pumping blood and adrenaline as news arrived of a building that had collapsed at the edge of town. Sixteen people—men, women, and children, were trapped beneath the rubble; onlookers could hear their cries for help.

The rescue teams at the center quickly geared up and were on the road in seconds.

Upon arriving at the scene, chaos reigned. Dust hung heavy in the air and the sounds of emergency sirens mixed with the frantic voices of rescue workers. The building lay in ruins, the wreckage casting shadows over the scene. It was a race against time, and the collective determination of the rescue teams and other first responders at the scene showed their commitment to saving everyone they could.

Max's senses were on high alert as he and Eliora made their way through the debris. His sharp nose guided them through gaps and openings, his paws skillfully navigating the uneven surfaces.

With each step, Eliora could feel Max's commitment, a shared purpose that bound them together.

Cries for help were still coming from beneath the rubble, a haunting reminder of the lives suspended in peril. The rescue teams moved precisely, their training and expertise guiding their actions. As Max and Eliora progressed, it was as if a silent understanding passed between them. Max's intuition directed him to areas others might not have looked at, and Eliora followed his lead.

The teams worked in rotation for close to 24 hours to continue the search without pause. Fatigue tugged at their muscles, but their determination remained unyielding. The families of the missing individuals waited anxiously, their faces etched with hope and fear. The emotional toll of the situation was evident, with the weight of the unknown hanging heavy in the air.

Eliora and Max had concluded their search of an area. They were on their way out when Max abruptly stopped and tilted his head in a gesture that conveyed that he sensed something, Eliora released Max from his harness. She followed his rapid movements across the debris-strewn landscape. His purposeful pace led to an area that had been meticulously searched and declared clear.

However, Max was insistent; he circled and darted around a specific spot as if driven by an unseen force. Recognizing the situation's urgency, Eliora urgently called for backup, her voice cutting through the din of rescue efforts. The team quickly decided to breach what seemed to be a solid wall, and as the first cracks appeared in the brick structure, a wave of disbelief washed over the team. Amid the jagged edges and rubble, they discovered a tear-streaked face—the features of a young girl. She had been nestled within the wall, concealed by the wreckage. Astonishment swept through the rescue team as they extended their arms and lifted the girl into the light.

STORY 4

Scent of Hope:

The Search for a Missing Soul

Chapter 1

Cheryl's breath caught in her throat, a jolt of raw fear coursing through her veins as she stared at her front door. A shiver raced down her spine, and unease swelled within her. The door, standing ajar, seemed to exhale a silent warning, setting off blaring alarm bells in her mind.

Her footsteps quickened as she darted into the house. Grocery bags slipped from her grasp, thudding onto the kitchen counter as her urgency grew. "Grandpa?" Her voice trembled with anxiety and hope as she called out, the echoes of her words swallowed by the ominous silence.

No response. The silence that followed was heavy and suffocating. Dread crept into Cheryl's veins, tightening its grip with every heartbeat.

She bounded up the stairs two at a time, the floorboards creaking beneath her frantic steps. The door to her grandpa's bedroom beckoned, and she pushed it open, her breath suspended in her chest as the scene unfolded before her. The room, bathed in muted light, greeted her with an eerie emptiness. Her heart sank as the truth settled in – her grandfather, a cornerstone of her world, was conspicuously absent, the room holding no trace of him.

Panic knotted in Cheryl's chest as she retraced her steps, a growing unease tightening its grip on her. She rushed through the house, checking every room, desperately hoping to find her grandfather somewhere. But it was as if he had vanished into thin air.

With her heart pounding, she bolted out the front door and crossed the lawn to Harold's house next door. Harold was her grandfather's chess mate, a kind and familiar face in their neighborhood. She pounded on his door, anxiety gnawing at her. When Harold opened the door, surprise across his face at her distressed expression.

"Cheryl, what's wrong?" Harold's voice was laced with concern.

Tears welled up in Cheryl's eyes as she blurted out, "Harold, have you seen my grandpa? He's not home, and I can't find him anywhere."

Harold's brow furrowed, and he stepped onto the porch, glancing worriedly toward Cheryl's house. "I haven't seen him, Cheryl. When did you last see him?"

Cheryl's voice trembled as she explained how she had left him napping earlier. Together, they began knocking on the doors of neighboring houses, inquiring if anyone had spotted him. But the answers were all the same – no one had seen or heard from him.

It was official: Mr. Granger had gone missing.

As the sinking feeling of dread intensified, Cheryl's trembling fingers dialed the number for the local police. Her voice quivered as she explained the situation, her words punctuated by anxious pauses. The dispatcher assured her that they would send an officer to her location.

Soon enough, sirens pierced the air as a police car approached her cottage. Cheryl rushed to meet the officer, her voice shaking as she recounted the events. The officer's expression was understanding as he jotted down notes and reassured her that they would initiate a search.

The search and rescue team arrived shortly afterwards. Eliora and Max were part of the search and rescue team that came to help.

Eliora went over to hug Cheryl.

"I'm sorry to hear this, Cheryl, but we'll find him," Eliora said, her voice laced with determination.

Cheryl's heart clenched with worry as the search and rescue team fanned out through the town. She watched as Eliora and Max headed towards the woods close by. It was well-known that her grandfather enjoyed long walks in those woods, a place where he found solace. However, Grandpa's mind was no longer what it used to be. In those moments when he lost touch with reality, he did things that could endanger him. Today was one of those days. Cheryl hoped with all her might that her grandfather was doing well.

Chapter 2

Hours passed, and the chill of the night wrapped around the search parties made up of the search and rescue teams and volunteers from the immediate neighborhood.

They had been searching for hours, calling out his name, and there had been no response so far. As the night deepened, the search continued, fueled by a sense of duty and desperation. The dogs involved in the search could feel the desperation of the search parties.

The moonlight played hide and seek with the treetops, casting shadows that danced around the searchlights they carried to light their way. But despite the darkness, their determination remained steadfast.

The goal was simple: find Mr. Granger.

The hours stretched on, and exhaustion began to take its toll. The air grew colder, and their breaths came out in visible puffs. The woods remained shrouded in an eerie stillness, save for the distant echoes of their calls and the rustling of leaves.

And then, suddenly, Max stopped in his tracks.

Attuned to his every move, Eliora also stopped and whispered, "What is it, Max? Do you sense something?'

A faint sound had reached Max's ears like a whisper in the wind—a soft scent that sent a jolt of recognition through him.

Sensing he was on to something, Eliora released him with a soft command, 'Go buddy,' and he was off in a flash.

Eliora was right behind him, and others close by followed as well. In seconds, word circulated that Max had caught a scent, and everyone was racing after Max. Some called for him to slow down, but he didn't. If anything, he went faster.

Instinct took over as Max sprinted in the direction of the river. The scent grew stronger with every stride, guiding him through the darkness. He could hear the bark of the other dogs behind him, along with the worried voices of his other friends, but he couldn't stop. Mr. Granger needed help, and Max's heart beat like a drum in his chest as he approached the riverbank.

There, on the edge of a fallen log, was Mr. Granger. His eyes were wide with fear, his fingers gripping the wet wood, holding on for dear life. Without thinking, Max launched himself into the water, the coldness of it hitting him like a hammer. The current tugged at him, but he was determined.

Max reached Mr. Granger just before he lost his grip, and with a desperate lunge he managed to catch hold of Mr. Granger's collar. The water was icy and the water fast-running and Max struggled to keep their heads above the surface as it pulled at them both. Mr. Granger's weight, the force of the water—it was a battle Max was determined to win.

The next wave hit them, throwing Max off balance, but he fought to regain his footing. The current roared in his ears, and for a moment, he feared it would consume them. Right when the waves were almost overwhelming, something happened. Someone grabbed hold of Max, and another grabbed Mr. Granger and started pulling them out of the water.

At that point, Max let go of Mr. Granger and looked up to see that Roland, the leader of the search and rescue team, was the one who had helped him. Another member held on to Mr. Granger, and together, they all made their way to the bank of the river.

They were battered and exhausted, but they were alive.

As the first light of dawn began to paint the sky, a new day emerged—one that carried a story of courage, unity, and the unwavering bonds that can weather any challenge.

On the other side of the woods, the hours seemed to stretch endlessly as the town braced itself for an outcome no one wanted to imagine. The sun had set, and the long shadows appeared to mirror the heaviness in Cheryl's heart. Neighbors offered their support, gathering to provide comfort and assistance in any way they could.

Suddenly, the receiver held by the officer who had stayed back with her crackled to life, and Eliora's voice floated over the receiver.

"We've found him."

A cheer went up from all those who were there.

Relief filled Cheryl's veins, her eyes welling up with tears as all the fear and anxiety that had flooded her body instantly drained.

About half an hour later, the search party emerged from the woods, and among them was her grandfather, disheveled but alive.

Cheryl rushed forward, enveloping him in a tight embrace. Tears streamed down her face as she held onto him, feeling a mixture of joy and gratitude that words could not express.

She looked at Eliora with tearful eyes and whispered, "Thank you,"

Eliora offered a warm smile, her bond with Max reflecting the connection between Cheryl and her grandfather. "We're here to help."

STORY 5

HEROES AMONG US

A Canine Hero's Tale of Triumph and Tragedy

Chapter 1

Eliora awoke that morning with an unsettling feeling. A cloud of unease hung heavy over her, as though the universe were whispering warnings directly into her soul. Every nerve in her body tingled with an unexplainable sense of impending doom, urging her to stay put and lock away the world outside. But she couldn't succumb to such irrational fears, could she?

By the time Eliora picked up Max from Brett's house, the sense of unease had grown stronger. An unsettling chill traced her spine as she drove to work, the sensation growing stronger with each passing mile. She brushed off her concerns, scolding herself for entertaining such thoughts. What harm could come on a beautiful day like this?

Eliora walked into the search and rescue headquarters to meet an atmosphere of suspense. The place was bustling with a sense of urgency, and the tension in the air was palpable. There had been reports of a nearby town that had suffered severely from a storm, leaving people in danger and buildings destroyed. Volunteers were urgently needed, and Eliora's sense of dread deepened – her earlier feeling of something terrible happening was now becoming an absolute and ominous truth.

The search and rescue teams mobilized quickly.

Eliora and Max found themselves amidst a chaotic symphony of emergency responders, each note played by the urgency of life and death. Their journey to the afflicted town was fraught with tension, a quiet acknowledgement of the dangerous task ahead.

Upon arrival, Eliora's pulse quickened as they beheld the aftermath of nature's fury. Destruction and despair painted a grim landscape. Multiple teams were hurrying to and fro to help those in need.

The search and rescue teams were already sifting through the destruction in search of survivors. Max's eager energy was undeniable, a stark contrast to the somber scene.

Shortly after they arrived, they were assigned a location to start working at.

Navigating the labyrinthine wreckage, Max's every step was measured and purposeful. Eliora mirrored his concentration, her heart pounding in rhythm with his pawbeats. The chaos around them was overwhelming, and each movement was a dance with danger, a reminder of the thin line between life and devastation.

A few moments later, Eliora's fears came to a head most dreadfully.

It all happened like a scene from a horror movie.

As she and Max carefully made their way through the rubble, his senses honed in on a faint cry, a desperate plea for salvation buried beneath the rubble's weight. The urgency electrified the air, and Max's focus intensified, his very being dedicated to the life that hung in the balance.

But as they continued searching, a chilling twist of fate unfolded. Max, her steadfast partner, suddenly disappeared into the chaos.

One second, he was there sniffing around, and the next, it was as though the ground under his feet shifted, and he disappeared with a heartwrenching whine of fear.

Eliora's heart seized, her scream echoing in the void that swallowed Max. Panic surged through her veins, her breath hitching in her throat. Time came to a stop as she dove towards where she last saw him, desperately calling his name over and over again.

"Max! Max! Maaaaaax!"

There was no response.

Chapter 2

Brett's day started like any other – peaceful, uneventful, and removed from the unpredictable chaos of search and rescue missions. He was enjoying a moment of tranquility, absorbed in a book, when his phone pierced the silence with its shrill ring. Frowning, he answered, and the world around him seemed to blur as he heard words that shattered his calm.

"Accident... Max..... injured......unresponsive."

The words struck Brett like a bolt of lightning, sending a surge of dread coursing through his veins. His grip on the phone tightened as he struggled to comprehend the gravity of the situation.

Max, his faithful partner, his source of purpose and strength, was hurt.

Brett felt his world tilt on its axis as his thoughts raced in different directions.

He could hear Eliora crying in the background as the person giving him details carried on, but all he could hear were those words:

"Accident... Max..... injured......unresponsive."

Every heartbeat felt like a drum, echoing the urgency of the moment. Brett's hands trembled as he dialed David and Lucy's numbers, and his voice choked with emotion as he conveyed the news. Their bond ran deep, forged in the shared experiences of joy and sorrow, and he knew they would share in his anguish.

Time became a blur as Brett wheeled himself out of his home, the urgency propelling him forward. The usually familiar surroundings felt distant and foreign as he made his way to his car. The engine roared to life, a reflection of his racing heart, and he sped towards the veterinary clinic.

With every mile he drove, thoughts of Max dominated his mind: Max's strength, his spirit and unwavering loyalty.

Images of the good times they had shared flashed through his mind as he drove.

The road ahead seemed endless, each second an eternity as he imagined the worst. He yearned for the moment when he would see Max again, but at the same time, fear gnawed at his heart.

Was the past going to repeat itself?

Was he destined to go through more pain and loss?

There were no answers in sight.

Brett's heart was a symphony of hope and fear as he approached the clinic. He saw Eliora's vehicle parked outside, a lifeline connecting him to his beloved Max.

The clinic's entrance loomed before them, a threshold to an uncertain fate. Brett parked the car with an urgency that matched his racing thoughts. He made his way to the reception to inquire about Max and was directed to a room where he found Eliora sitting and staring blankly at the far wall.

When she saw him, she seemed to crumble into herself and begin weeping again. Without a word, he moved closer and held her. Between sobs, she told him everything that had happened from when she woke up until the accident. She blamed herself for everything.

Though he was just as worried as she was, he tried to be strong for all of them.

He sat there beside her, with her head on his shoulder, trying to console her, and that was how Lucy and David found them.

Together, they waited for Max, who was in surgery.

Chapter 3

The air inside the clinic seemed heavy with anticipation as Brett, Eliora, Lucy, and David sat in the waiting room, each heartbeat echoing the uncertainty of the situation. Time seemed to stretch into eternity until the door to the surgery swung open. The doctor emerged, his expression a mix of gravity and relief, a beacon of hope in a sea of anxiety.

Brett's heart leapt at the sight of the doctor, his grip on Eliora's hand tightening. The moment of truth had arrived, he needed answers.

"Are you Max's family?" the doctor asked gently, his eyes conveying sympathy and professionalism.

Brett nodded, his voice momentarily escaping as he fought to steady his emotions. Eliora's grip on his hand offered silent reassurance, a shared strength in the face of uncertainty.

The doctor's gaze settled on them, his demeanor a blend of empathy and professionalism. "Max sustained significant injuries in the fall," he began, his words measured as he walked them through the details. "He has fractures in both hind legs, a dislocated shoulder, and some trauma to his back."

Brett's heart seemed to skip a beat as the weight of Max's injuries settled over him. The words 'both legs' brought back memories of another time when those words crushed his entire future and completely altered the course of his life.

Was the past going to repeat itself? Again, Brett was reminded of how fragile life is.

The doctor continued, his tone both informative and compassionate. "The good news is that Max is out of surgery and stable. We've fixed his fractures and addressed the dislocation. He's a strong dog, and his vital signs are encouraging."

A surge of relief washed over Brett as the doctor's words offered a glimmer of hope. Max's strength, the same strength that had led them through countless missions, seemed to shine through even in this moment of vulnerability.

The doctor's gaze held theirs, and his voice was steady as he explained the road ahead. "However, the injuries are extensive. Max will need time to heal and won't be able to work for the next few months. The initial phase of his recovery will require close monitoring and care."

Brett's mind raced, and his heart was a flurry of conflicting emotions. The road to recovery would be a journey, one that would test their patience and resilience. But knowing that Max would be fine, that his life had been spared, was a balm for Brett's worried soul.

"We'll need to keep him on restricted activity for the first few days," the doctor continued, his gaze kind. "And I'd advise regular follow-up visits to monitor his progress."

Eliora's grip tightened on Brett's hand, her expression a mirror of his own mixed emotions. Max's resilience, which had led him through countless missions, had once again proven its worth.

The doctor's presence offered a comforting reassurance, a beacon of light amid uncertainty. As they absorbed the information, a sense of gratitude filled the air, a shared understanding that they had been given another chance to hold onto the precious bond they shared with Max.

Brett's heart swelled with relief and gratitude, his voice finding its strength. "Thank you, Doctor," he said, his words carrying the weight of his emotions. "Thank you for taking care of him."

As they looked ahead to the road to recovery, the journey seemed daunting yet filled with hope. Max's strength had led them through countless trials before, and as they navigated this new challenge, they knew their unbreakable bond would be their guiding light.

Chapter 4

Sometimes, it's easy to take the everyday heroes who walk among us for granted. They quietly go about their tasks, leaving a trail of positive impact in their wake, often unnoticed until circumstances take a turn for the unexpected. This was especially true for Max, the search and rescue dog who had become an inseparable part of the town's tapestry of life.

As news of Max's injury rippled through the town, it was as if the collective breath of the community caught in their throats. Max's name had become synonymous with courage, a four-legged embodiment of hope who had fearlessly navigated danger to save lives. The stories of his heroism spread like wildfire, touching the hearts of both young and old, bridging gaps between neighbors, and creating bonds that defied the ordinary.

Max's unwavering dedication and the countless lives he had saved had woven themselves into the very fabric of the town's identity. Every child who had returned to their parents and every family member who had reunited with their loved ones due to Max's efforts owed a debt of gratitude to his exceptional abilities.

Yet, it wasn't until that fateful day, when Max's life was in the balance, that the town truly comprehended the extent of his impact. As news of his injury spread, it was as if a curtain had been drawn, revealing the underlying threads of appreciation and admiration Max had woven into the people's hearts.

With every call, visit, card, bouquet, and toy that found its way to Brett's home, it became more and more evident that Max's influence was far-reaching. Every well-wisher who stopped by, every gesture of support carried a story of a life touched by Max's actions. Strangers shared tales of rescue missions, recounting moments when hope seemed lost, only to be rekindled by Max's determined efforts.

Neighbors who had never spoken beyond the occasional wave left heartfelt notes expressing their gratitude for the peace of mind Max had brought to the town. The walls of Brett's home became a canvas of connection, painted with the brushstrokes of stories that showcased the extent to which Max had impacted lives in the community.

Eliora's involvement in Max's recovery extended beyond the surface with each passing day. She seamlessly integrated herself into Brett's life, offering a steady presence that brought comfort and a sense of belonging. Her genuine concern for Max's well-being was matched only by her growing fondness for Brett. Their interactions transcended the ordinary, evolving into conversations that effortlessly flowed from the mundane to the profound.

Riding along to doctor's appointments, Eliora provided moral support and an attentive ear for Brett's concerns. Once a place of medical necessity, the veterinary clinic became a space where their connection deepened. Eliora's understanding of medical jargon and her ability to translate complex terms into simple explanations made her an invaluable ally in Max's recovery journey.

As Max's strength returned and he was ready for more activity, Eliora eagerly stepped in to assist with his care. Their walks became a shared ritual, an opportunity for Max to stretch his muscles and for Eliora and Brett to share moments of lightheartedness. The once-formal visits transformed into strolls where laughter and stories flowed freely, weaving the fabric of their growing bond.

Mealtimes became occasions to relish each other's company. The shared dinners brought a sense of warmth and intimacy, creating a space where Eliora and Brett could be themselves, unguarded and unfiltered. As they exchanged anecdotes, their connection grew, their chemistry undeniable.

During Max's recovery, the foundation for a new relationship was laid. The mutual respect, empathy, and shared experiences formed a bond that transcended the heroics of Max's rescue missions. Eliora's presence in Brett's life brought a sense of completeness he hadn't realized was missing. And as they navigated the ups and downs of Max's journey to full recovery, the lines between friendship and something more began to blur.

Overall, Max's absence served as a reminder of the void he had filled – not just as a skilled search and rescue dog but as a symbol of hope, resilience, and the extraordinary capacity for animals to touch human hearts. The town discovered that heroes weren't limited to those with capes and masks; sometimes, they wore fur coats and wagging tails.

And as the day approached when Max would return to his duties, the town stood ready to welcome him back with open arms and hearts full of appreciation. Sometimes, it takes a moment of vulnerability to understand the magnitude of one's impact, and Max's injury illuminated the depths of his significance in the most unexpected way.

In the end, it was undeniable: Max was a hero.

Conclusion

I hope you have enjoyed our journey with Max, our loyal and loving guide through the vibrant, rolling meadows of life's experiences. It is my deepest hope that Max has become as real to you as he is to me, and that his tales have warmed your heart just as the living, breathing companions of my youth warmed mine.

I am extremely grateful that you chose to wander these paths with us. With every page you turned, you breathed life into these stories, allowing Max and his world to exist not only in my memories but in the present, in the hearts and minds of readers like you.

As you finish this book, I hope you carry with you not just the stories themselves, but the essence of Max—his loyalty, his love, his indefatigable spirit. I hope he reminds you of every dog that has left a paw print on your heart and that his stories have stirred in you the comforting, familiar love that only a true canine companion can offer.

Thank you, from the bottom of my heart, for reading and for allowing Max and the love he symbolizes to become a part of your world. I am honoured that you have walked this journey with us and that, in these pages, you found a touch of the joy and companionship that the dogs of my past so generously gave to me.

This book was my humble gift of gratitude for the happiness that the dogs of my life, especially Max, brought into my existence. And your reading—your time, your emotional investment—has been the most treasured gift back.

-       *Grace Kenny*

Made in United States
Orlando, FL
29 August 2024

50911598R00043